Escape from Dorsester Street

THE RED PLUME PRESS

The Red Plume Press
Petrolia, Ontario, Canada

Escape
from
Dorsester
Street

A novel
by

Gerry Van Hoorn

Escape
from
Dorsester
Street

Gerry Van Hoorn

First Print Edition May 2018

Copyright © Gerry Van Hoorn 2012

ISBN: 978-1775362401

Dedication

This is my first book written in
the English language.

Dedicated to the memory
of my daughter,
Marjolein.

Preface

It was still early in the morning and some of the women were so-called 'ready for business'. When William came riding his bicycle on the street where these ladies were working, he had to go past one of them to go to his office. She called out him, "Hey buddy, would you please do something for me?"

Surprised and not knowing what to say, he went over to the lady. The day had just begun and she was already looking tired. She asked him, "Please, could you take out the trashcan for me? It is in the back of the house. Don't be afraid I am not going to hurt you." He went to the back of the house to get the trashcan and brought it to the curb. She smiled at him and he hurried off to his office in the building next door. A co-worker had been watching him and asked, "Do you know that lady?" Some people always think that they are funny. William shrugged his shoulders and did not answer.

He could not forget the sadness in the face of the woman. What a miserable life it must be to have to lay down your life for the pleasure of men! The one who would take all your money at the end of the day is the man who would treat you harshly when you cannot come up with the money he thinks that you owe him.

From the office you could see the women, most of them standing or sitting in the front of the window, waiting for customers. Sometimes their pimps came by to check to make sure the ladies were working. You could see that these pimps were mean and intolerant of their women.

William felt sorry and never understood how a woman could choose a life like that. Once in a week, the Salvation Army came to the street to sing and pray for these ladies, much to the dismay of the pimps. The pimps could not do anything about it because it is a public street.

There were not always sad stories to tell. For instance, sometimes men were standing at the corner and just watching the women. Then someone would shout out of the window from the office, "Hey, the bus stop is around the corner!"

One comes to the realization that there will always be slaves. People choose their own destiny...or could it be different?

So, this is the story of Jennifer. All names of persons and places are fictional but part of the story, as I have been told, is real.

Chapter 1

Jennifer, a two-year-old girl, with blond hair and blue eyes, was running through the corridor of the big apartment house. She looked at the many doors and thought they looked spooky. To the little girl, the house was like a castle. The house had only three floors. The lights in the corridors were always "on" because the windows were only at the end of each corridor. Sometimes Jennifer could look outside and see the park across the road. The house was in a downtown neighborhood, on a busy street of the city called Blytonfille. The city was on the Blue River and in a busy industrial area.

Jennifer's mother was not home. She worked in a grocery store, and an old lady took care of Jennifer. Jennifer's mother rented one of the apartments on the second floor. Many strange people were living in the house and some of them were scary looking. There was a tall black man, of whom Jennifer was not afraid, because he had friendly eyes and always had a friendly smile. He was so tall that she always had to look up to him like a big giant.

When he saw her, he never missed the chance to say, "Hi little girl! How are you?" The old lady who took care of her knew this black man and sometimes she spoke to him in a familiar way. Jennifer grew up quickly, and things in the big house changed. The people living in the house were still the same except the tall black man was gone. She never asked where he had gone. The old lady stopped taking care of Jennifer because the lady became sick and went into a nursing home.

Jennifer realized that her mother had changed and that a strange man was making her cry. Her mother told her that she had to work for this man and that he was her father. Jennifer could not understand why he was her father because she had never seen him before. When she was in grade school, she'd asked many questions about this man, but her life had gone on without answers or seeing this so-called father. Now that she was a teenager, things changed again. Often her mother came home late and cried softly at night.

One night the strange man came into their room and looked at Jennifer. He said to her mother, "That girl will be a beauty and will make lots of money." Jennifer was scared and could not sleep. What did he mean by that?

A year later Jennifer was home from school doing her homework when her mother came home with' her father' and a few more men. You could see that her mother had been beaten again. Her face was swollen and she could not use her arm. The men were rough and loud-mouthed and were looking at Jennifer.

Jennifer felt uncomfortable and one of the men came over to her. He put his hand on her leg and she pushed him away. Her mother looked terrified but did not try to protect her daughter. Jennifer got away from the man and fled the room. She left the building, ran to the variety store around the corner where she knew a lady that she could trust, who worked there. The lady knew that Jennifer's mother was a prostitute and she talked with Jennifer about it. She knew the danger and told Jennifer that she could always come to her when she was in trouble.

Later, after the men were gone, Jennifer went back home. Her mother was making dinner and Jennifer asked her why she had been beaten and why she allowed such abuse. Her mother told her to shut up and not to make any more trouble. Jennifer asked her mother why they had to stay with her so-called father? Her mother answered that he was her husband that she had to obey him. Jennifer knew from that time on that her mother was a slave and was afraid of losing her life.

The man was Chuck Bentons, an ex-criminal, who last year had been released from jail. He had married Alice, Jennifer's mother. He was a mean person and his friends were the same type. They had no respect for human life. They lived above the law. At that time, as now, money could buy you a crooked lawyer. Men could get way with abuse and a woman had no form of protection, by the law or any other organization. Women were not able to find shelter from that kind of evil; even the law took a blind eye to the criminal activities of men using their wives as their source of income. Police at that time were not able to protect prostitutes from inhumane treatment. Some police were bought with money or other favors, to look the other way, as they were often friends of these men. The hope was that in the future all of this would change. Many organizations were lobbying for that change but for Jennifer and her mother, it would come too late. Alice would remain the slave of an evil man who had no

5

conscience. For Jennifer, born of a mother in slavery, there could be a chance for a better life.

Chapter 2

Jennifer was still attending high school and this was her last year. She knew that she would be graduating with good marks because she was one of the better students in her class. The school was one of the best in the neighborhood of the city, built only a few years ago. There were many sports facilities and one of them was the great Olympic size and style swimming pool. The pool was always busy and Jennifer had always wanted to be on the school swimming team because she was a good swimmer but was not allowed to take part in any competition. Her excuse was always that she could not afford to pay for it. The school was even willing to let Jennifer compete for free, but her mother still did not allow her to participate in any competition other than in school. Many of Jennifer's friends in her class knew what was going on in her life. They were sorry for what she had to endure. Their parents were afraid to take action or to warn the police for their own safety.

One day when Jennifer came home from school, her mother was not there but some men were in the room. She could hear their voices. She became frightened and before she could walk away, she was pulled in the room.

Her father and the men were all over her and she knew what they were going to do. She started screaming for help and her voice was heard through the whole house. A lady upstairs was yelling that she was going to call the police. The men were losing their grip on her and she managed to escape out of the door. She was running through the street until she reached the variety store. When she entered the store, she could not see the lady normally there. A different person was working and Jennifer was disappointed not to have the help she normally would have.

The person in the store told her that the lady, Jennifer was looking for, was in the hospital and she did not know where the lady was living. He was feeling sorry for Jennifer and asked her if he could help her. Jennifer not knowing what to do, said thanks and went out of the store. She could not go home so she decided to go to one of her friend's home. Later she went home and before she opened the door, she made sure nobody was there. She went to bed without dinner and she cried and prayed that nothing else would happen to her. But she did not know that the worst was still to come.

The whole week she was hoping to see the lady from the variety store but she did not show up. Jennifer's mother (Alice) did not speak to her and Jennifer was hoping that she would tell her what she could do to help her or to protect her. Why could she not leave with Jennifer? They can go to another city or hide somewhere with friends. But then she realized that she had never seen her mother with other people. It was Jennifer's birthday and her mother had never given her a present or even wished her a happy birthday. She did not understand why she was treated that way. Sometimes friends from school gave her a party and took Jennifer to an ice-cream parlor for a treat but not this year. Jennifer wished that she had family to go to. She knew that she had none.

That dreadful Saturday night, her father came home

drunk. The alcohol was strong on his breath. Normally that was the best thing for Jennifer because her father always fell asleep when he was drunk. But not that night, he was looking at Jennifer in a strange way and she tried not to look at him. She was so afraid of this man.

Her father had something in his hand that she could not see what. He asked her to bring him a glass of water. When she was close to him, he stood up and put his arm around her neck and at the same time, he put a cloth against her mouth. Jennifer struggled to get loose but she lost her strength and lost consciousness.

When she woke up there was a strange man standing over her and she knew what he was going to do to her. Jennifer knew she was not capable of defending herself but she cried and begged the man to go away and not to harm her.

The man was smiling while he took off his belt. He told her to relax and said, "You will enjoy our little play but first, I will teach you to obey!" He hit her with his belt and she could not do anything other than cry.

The man then raped her and when her mother entered the room, she saw that Jennifer was severely beaten. She looked at her daughter with empty eyes, without emotion and did nothing to help her. The man said to Jennifer, "From now on you have to work for me and do what I tell you. You understand?"

When the man was gone, Jennifer cried and could not sleep that night. It was still dark and her mother was sleeping when she left the room with a few personal belongings. It was quiet in the corridors as most people in

9

the building were asleep. She left the house quietly through the back door, hoping that nobody would notice her. The back door opened into a dark and narrow alley. There was the smell of garbage and she had to be careful where she was walking so as not to make any noise. She was not concerned that anybody would be in the alley.

She walked along the street towards the bus station. There was always a place to sleep or hide there. Close to the far corner of one of the side streets, a man was coming her way. There was a house close by and Jennifer walked over to the entrance of the house. The house had a small-unlit hallway so luckily nobody could see her. When the man had passed the house, she could see it was the same man who had raped her earlier that night. A cold chill went through her body but she kept quiet until she could not hear his footsteps anymore. She prayed that the man was gone and she began to cry. Then she heard a voice of a woman behind her and a door opened. A dim light entered the doorway and she could she the woman. Jennifer must have bumped into the door and had made the lady look who was at the door.

Both looked at each other and the woman asked her to step inside. She called her husband and said; "Please Jim come here and look at this girl". The man called Jim was a tall man with friendly eyes and he looked upon Jennifer. He asked her, "Dear girl, what happened to you?" Jennifer began to cry again and could not speak right away. The only thing she could do was shiver and cry.

After she was seated in a chair, the man looked carefully at her and said, "I know you. You are Jennifer from the old big house at Dorsester Street. What in heaven happened to you, girl?"

Now Jennifer was not afraid and somehow, she knew this man was a good man. She quietly told him what had happened to her. The lady told Jennifer that she must stay at their house. She asked Jennifer if she was hungry or if she needed something to drink. Her husband was helping to make a bed for her. Before Jennifer could go to bed the lady told her she would first take care of her medical condition. The lady wanted to make sure that she had no injuries other than the marks from her beating. The lady told Jennifer that her name was Ellis and her husband's name was Jim and that she was a nurse from the Wood Hospital. Jim and Ellis had come home just a few minutes earlier because they had been working late.

Jennifer needed a bath and Ellis would take care of her but first she took a sample of the sperm for later evidence. She gave Jennifer the same treatment in the same way as they did in the hospital when a woman was raped. Ellis then asked her if she would like to stay at their home. She would to talk to her husband about how they could help her because she obviously could not go back home. Jennifer said, "Please let me stay. I am so afraid!"

When she went to her bed, she could not sleep right away. Too many things went through her mind. She had heard so many things from girls in school about sickness and pregnancy. She prayed, "Please God, help me!"

Ellis spoke to her husband about Jennifer. Jim told Ellis Jennifer's mother and her profession. They decided to take the risk and responsibility to take care of Jennifer.

First of all, she could not go out of the house and could not have any contact with other people. The people who wanted to do harm to Jennifer would be able to find her. Jim told his wife that as long as Jennifer was 16 years of age then there would be no legal consequences for the both of them and that they should find a way to help Jennifer.

Jim Lester was thinking of Jennifer when she was a little girl. It was 12 years ago that he left the house at Dorsester Street. Two months later, he met Ellis in the hospital. Jim was a clerk at the hospital for 15 years and had never dated a woman. Shortly after he met Ellis, they married and they bought the house at West Street. They discovered that Ellis could not have children of her own. She loved children and felt a warmth inside to have a chance to take care of Jennifer.

There were a lot of problems to take care of. It was not possible to take the girl outside or even let her stand in the front of the window. People are always curious and like to know what is going on in their neighborhood. The next day, Ellis told Jennifer that she and her husband were going to help her. When she asked Jennifer how old she was, Jennifer told her that she was 16 and that her birthday was two weeks ago, Ellis was delighted and happy, as this meant Jennifer could stay with no legal repercussions. She told Jennifer that she could not go to school and that she had to stay inside the house for at least a week. Ellis reminded Jennifer not to contact anyone, not to open the door or even look out of the window. Nobody could know that she was in the house. Jim would come home at lunch-time and would check up on her.

After a couple of days, Ellis was getting used to having the girl in her house but she knew that it could not be for long. Jim and Ellis were planning for Jennifer to stay somewhere else where she would be safe. It would cost them quite a bit of money, but they were decided in their plan. Jennifer had to go as far away as possible from where they were living, at best in another city.

Jim and Ellis Lester had friends in Massonville who also had no children of their own either, so it would be perfect. Ellis told Jim that she would take a few days vacation and she could take Jennifer to Massonville. There she would talk to their friends about the situation. Jim was not so happy with his wife's idea. When Jim was back in his office in the hospital, he made a discreet phone call to Massonville.

That Friday, everything was settled. Early in the morning, Jim drove his wife and Jennifer to the bus station where they took the bus to Massonville. Jennifer was dressed like a boy with her hair was tucked under a woolen cap so nobody would accidentally recognize her. While on the bus they had little or no conversation, speaking only when necessary. They had to travel two hours to take a transfer to another bus.

During the trip, Ellis was looking at Jennifer. She noticed that the girl was average looking but not bad looking either. She thought about the things that had happened to the girl and she almost had to cry again.

The travel went without any problems and there were not many people on the bus. Later, they ate the lunch they had brought with them. Around midnight, they arrived in

Massonville, where they took a cab to the street close to where the friends of Jim and Ellis lived. This was just for security so that nobody would know the address. When they arrived at the home, the door opened up and they were hurried inside.

The lady of the house was a pretty woman who had a lovely smile. Ellis introduced Jennifer to Mrs. Conny Stuart and then they went into the living room where all things were discussed. Conny asked if Jennifer would like to stay with her and her husband. Jennifer really had no choice and she had no idea what else to do. She really liked Ellis and she could not leave her so easily. But Ellis knew what was going through the young girl's head and she would never leave her if she thought that their friends were incapable of taking care of her. Conny was always like a sister to Ellis, and her husband did everything to please his wife.

Ellis stayed that night at the Stuarts' home. That night they talked over all the rules and responsibilities, of Jennifer's stay at the home of Vince and Conny. She would stay there as long as necessary. Ellis and Jim would pay for clothes, and the cost of the girl's stay with the Stuarts. Conny showed Jennifer her new bedroom and the rest of the house. Later that night Vince Stuart came home from work and they all got to talking about the future.

Of course, they knew that Jennifer should first finish her schooling so that she would have a good education and later be able to apply for a job. She could not go to a school in Massonville so it was decided that it would be better for Jennifer to take a correspondence course to finish her high school. The next day, Ellis said goodbye to Jennifer and Conny. Vince drove Ellis to the bus station, and after promising to take good care of the girl, they said goodbye. There would be no communication other than a phone call. Ellis was exhausted and could not keep her mind off the girl she had just left with her friends. When she returned home, Jim was eager to know how that everything went and they talked for a long time that night.

Chuck Bentons and his friend (the one who had raped Jennifer) were not happy about her disappearance. They suspected that Alice had something to do with it. But even by slapping Alice and treating her harshly, she could not tell them when or where she was gone. After almost a week, they started looking around in the neighborhood and asked the neighbours questions about whether they had seen Jennifer. They also showed a picture to the police and told Alice to put a photo in the local newspaper that she was looking for her. Chuck Bentons asked a police friend with a dog to trace the route Jennifer had taken but because it had rained for two days, they could not go further than the apartment building where they were living. Two weeks later they discontinued the search as they had no success.

In her heart Alice was happy that Jennifer had got away but was also scared about what may have happened to her daughter. She felt that she had been a coward and a worthless mother. She never stood up for herself and Jennifer.

Chapter 3

A new life was beginning for Jennifer. The house of Mr. and Mrs. Stuart was on a quiet street and they had no direct neighbors. There was a park and a shopping mall close by. Conny Stuart went shopping to buy some new clothes for Jennifer. When she came back home, they talked a lot and Conny had a good feeling about the relationship she was developing with Jennifer. Now she had a daughter and the former emptiness in her house would be filled with happiness. Her only concern was for Vince as he had always been number one in her life and she could not take that away from him. She need not have worried because Vince had no problem with the change in the house. Now they could talk about different sorts of things and he liked the way the women got along. He had a job that took him away from home, sometimes for a couple of days. He was glad to know that Conny would no longer be alone.

The next day, the women looked through the newspapers for a correspondence school. They also phoned the local school for other possibilities for Jennifer to be able to finish her last year in high school. The secretary from the high school needed more information and they told her that they would phone back later. The only possibility was to go with the correspondence school so Jennifer's identity would remain safe.

Before they made any decision, they talked it over with Vince that night at dinner. Vince had a better idea and suggested that Jennifer should take an exam right away.

Vince could get some books and the curriculum from the last year of high school. He knew a friend whose daughter was attending the local high school. So, they decided to go with Vince's plan. The next week Jennifer was studying at home and started having questions she could not ask a teacher but Conny was able to help her a lot.

The time seemed to fly. The days and weeks were going by fast. The women became best friends and when Vince came home, there was a lot to tell and to share. Vince was happy to see that the women could get along so well and he was thinking ahead to what would happen when the time came that Jennifer would have to leave. But that was still some ways off and he pushed the thought from his mind. Spring was in the air and Conny loved to work in the garden, so she had to leave Jennifer with her studies.

Graduation for Jennifer was to be that year and they had already applied for the necessary papers to take the state exam for high school. It was not always easy for Jennifer to keep her mind on the things she had to study because she was alone and she so wanted to go out of the house.

The Stuarts' house was small but comfortable. The house was located on a quiet street with little or no traffic. Lots of blossoming trees decorated the street and with the spring flowers, it was hard to stay inside! Conny worked almost every day in the garden. She planted new seeds for vegetables and flowers. The garden had a lovely setting and was enclosed by a wooden fence; a few trees surrounded the perimeter. So, it was a secluded area, quiet and frequented by lots of different birds. Jennifer loved to sit outside in the garden and to watch the little birds on the bird feeder but the study had to come first.

During the upcoming weekend, they were expecting a visit from Ellis and Jim. It had been a couple of months since they had been there the last time. Jennifer was looking forward to seeing them and to hear all the stories of what was happening in their town and of course, about her mother.

That night at dinner Vince was looking at Jennifer and noticed how she was becoming relaxed and that she looked healthier. It was a good feeling to see the girl so happy and he found himself wishing that she were his own daughter. But he did not know how to express his feelings for her. Vince decided to talk with Conny about it and she told him that she had the same feeling and that she did not want to think of the time when she would have to miss Jennifer. She told Vince that they could do something for her future by taking out life insurance or setting up a savings account. This would be some security for Jennifer so they decided to do so and they would talk about this with Ellis and Jim.

That weekend was filled with much joy and they all were thankful for the many things had they been able to accomplish. The friendship between the two couples was born many years ago when Ellis and Conny were dating Jim and Vince. They had met each other at a Christmas party from the hospital. Jim and Vince were already longtime friends through their school years. By hiding Jennifer, they had taken a big risk but they knew that they could trust each other. It was only to keep Jennifer away from her father. She could go her own way because of her age, but the influence her father had with criminals made her an easy target. Even the police at that time were corrupt so they still had to be very careful about Jennifer's safety.

The hospital was becoming busy and Jim and Ellis were unable to come for another visit. Jim had to work long hours. Before he did not mind doing so but now he wanted to be at home. Ellis phoned one night to say that there was a photo of Jennifer in the local paper with a message that her mother was looking for her. It really bothered Jim and Ellis but they did not know what to do. Everything had been going so well and Jennifer was ready to do her exam. Luckily, they had not sent in the papers yet. So, Jennifer couldn't be found through her exam papers but it still bothered Jim that Jennifer's mother was looking for her. What if there was something wrong with her mother?

That night Jim made a telephone call to Vince, asking to meet on the weekend so they could talk about it. That weekend Jim drove the car to Massonville and he was glad to be seeing his friends again. In his mind, he was praying for some good news. All the things were so good for Vince and his wife because of Jennifer. She was a blessing for his friends and that made him very happy.

The trip took a couple of hours and the ride over was quiet. Not much traffic for the time of the day. He did not drive too much by himself but he liked it that way because he didn't have to keep up a conversation. Jim was a loner and liked to keep things to himself. Being with Vince was different, though. He could trust Vince and they were the same kind of men. He could still remember the time they were in school together and all the good times they had had.

When Jim arrived in Massonville, Vince and Conny were already waiting for him. Both men kept silent until they were sitting drinking coffee. Conny looked worried and did not participate in the conversation until the men had theirs.

Jim had done some investigation on the whereabouts of Jennifer's mother. He had made a visit to the big house where he used to live and carefully had asked some questions. Jennifer's mother was still living there and the situation had not changed for her. The only thing that had changed was the state she was in. She had broken her arm twice in the last four months under suspicious circumstances and still she had to work as a prostitute. The man she was living with had become even more cruel in his behavior towards her. Jim told Vince not to worry and to keep Jennifer at their home until they could find out more information for him. The law would not do anything because as far as they knew, there was no crime involved and there was no missing person report made by anybody. Jennifer could do her exam anytime she wanted to. After lunch, they came to the conclusion not to do anything until things were safe for Jennifer.

Chapter 4

The night was cool and wet when Jennifer's mother decided to go home. She did not make any money that night. More and more competition from much younger girls made it very difficult for her. For the first time in her life, she did not want to live anymore. She had no friends and no family left. It was her own fault that she had lost her daughter because she was too afraid to try to protect her. The last couple of weeks, her husband had slapped her around and abused her more frequently because he thought that she knew where Jennifer was. She had told him that she had left in the middle of the night but he did still not believe her. In her heart, she was happy that Jennifer had got away.

Luckily, nobody was in the room when Alice opened the door to her apartment. She was not hungry but she knew she must cook for her husband. An idea came to her of how to defend herself this time from the cruelty she knew would be coming to her. She took a large kitchen knife and put it under her apron. Just in time, too, because the apartment door opened and her husband and his friend came inside.

She could hear that they were drunk. Her husband barged into the kitchen and gave her his everyday order to give him the money. She told him she'd made none. He became angry as this was the second day in a row that she didn't make him any money. He lunged at her and grabbed her by the throat. She began to choke but this time, she was prepared to defend herself. She clutched the knife she had hidden under her apron and stabbed her husband in the chest. Once, twice, three times she plunged the knife before he finally let her go. Without any noise, he collapsed to his knees and died.

His friend was sitting in a chair in the living room, watching the television, unaware of what had just happened in the kitchen. Alice knew this was her chance to take revenge for the rape of her daughter. The sound of the TV was loud and the man was sitting with his back to the kitchen. So, she silently walked over to him and stabbed the bloody knife into his throat and chest, killing him as well.

Both of these abusive men were dead. All of a sudden, she felt freedom and could sing and laugh, she was so relieved. She did not think of the consequences of what she had done and she did not care. She thought that her life was worthless anyway. She double-checked to make sure that both men were dead. Then, she took most, but not all, of their money and some valuables. The only thing she still wanted was the money her husband kept in a small safe. It belonged to her because she is the one that had worked for it. She could never open the safe because her husband had the key. But now she had the key! There were also some papers in the safe, but Alice did not care about that.

When she finally was ready, she left the apartment with a small package. It was addressed to a good friend at the local newspaper, along with a note to give the package to her daughter Jennifer whenever he found her. She asked him not to tell anybody about what she had given him. He

(Alex) was a good man and she could trust him. After she had delivered the package to the newspaper, she went to a small but good restaurant for a decent meal. She thought about Jennifer and worried about what had happened to her. But all of this was too late. She was not a worthy mother to Jennifer.

When she left the restaurant, it was already late in the night and she decided to go to the police station to confess what she had done. A few officers were in the station and they looked surprised when she came in. One of them, known by her husband, made a joke about her but when she told her story, they did not believe her at first. But this was no joke, they finally realized. Then the men escorted Alice to a cell and phoned the police chief. After that, everything went fast: the firemen and police cars surrounded the apartment building where the murders had happened.

Jennifer's mother went to prison while waiting for her trial. In prison, her life was a lot better; she had a regular meal and a safe place to be. The man from the newspaper came to visit and told her not to worry. He would stay in touch with her. He, Alexander, would try to find Jennifer and he promised her to help her in any way he could.

Jim came home from work and read the headline story in the newspaper with some relief and also with sadness. He told Ellis what had happened with Jennifer's mother, Alice. Now they had to tell Jennifer and that was not going to be easy. Did Jennifer still want to go to visit her mother? What would happen when the newspaper reporters find out about her? They had to be very careful.

Everybody at the house of Vince and Conny were surprised when Jim and Ellis came to visit. They had phoned ahead but did not tell the reason of their visit. Jim told Vince that he would like to have a word with him in private.

So, they went out in the garden and Jim told Vince what had happened with Jennifer's mother. Then the two of them discussed some possibilities in how to approach the situation.

They first had dinner and were relaxing with a cup of coffee when Jim told everyone else what the visit was all about. Conny and Jennifer were very quiet and both had different thoughts. Jennifer was scared and did not know what to think about all of this. Her life was so good here and she loved Conny more than her mother. She would not like to change her life but her mother was locked up in jail and maybe she was sick or lonely?

Conny was afraid to lose Jennifer as she was like the daughter she never had. She could not imagine what life would be like without her. This was too much for Conny to consider and she had to go upstairs to her bedroom.

Jim looked at Jennifer and told her that if she wanted to visit her mother, he would take her over to the jail, when the time was right. Ellis said that Jennifer must take some time to think about what she would like to do. In the meantime, Jim would try to visit Jennifer's mother in jail with the excuse that he was an old neighbour. Normally, they do not allow any visitors other than her lawyer. First, he would have to find out about her lawyer.

Jim was lost in thought about all these things on their way home. Ellis was quiet as well. Surprisingly, the ride home went by quickly and the weather was perfect. Jim was thinking about taking a vacation with Ellis this coming summer. They had been talking about it for a long time but now all that had to wait again. For the first time he was wondering if they had done the right thing with Jennifer but that thought was gone fast because he knew better inside. After a good night's sleep, Jim felt better and Ellis reassured him that he needn't worry.

At work he had no time to think about the problem because he was very busy. Many people came to the hospital with flu problems. He had not seen Ellis. When he came home he watched the latest local news in the hopes of finding out more about Jennifer's mother but there was nothing new to report. Jim was tired and had almost fallen asleep when Ellis came home. Her first question was "Did you hear any news?" but she knew from Jim's expression that there was no news yet. Their lives had gone from a dull, everyday routine to an anxious wait to find out what would unfold each day.

Ellis went to the kitchen to make a list of groceries she had to buy the next day. How she wanted a child of her own but it was too late for her. She was thinking of talking to Jim to find out what his thoughts were about adopting a child. She knew that a child would change their way of living and Ellis would have to stay at home. She realized that that was not possible so she brushed the idea out of her thoughts.

The flu season was in full swing; the hospital was overloaded with patients. In the coming days, Ellis and Jim were too busy to think about much of anything else. The prosecution was examining the murder case against Jennifer's mother. There were many questions about the situation. She had murdered two men and they wanted to know what made her do this. Doctors were examining Alice and were aware of the abuse done by her husband, but because she was a prostitute nothing could be proven without any witnesses. Alice decided to keep as many things related to her daughter secret and would not reveal anything that might bring her daughter into danger. She told the prosecution that her daughter Jennifer had run away from home when she was 16 years old and that she never had any contact with her after that. Another question she was asked was what she knew about any money.

When Alice had taken the money out of the small safe before she left, she had put the key back in the pocket of her dead husband. In the safe there were some papers but she did not touch them and she made sure not to talk about that either. After a week-long questioning, Alice was appointed a lawyer. She could not afford a good and experienced lawyer so she had to rely on Mr. Stanton. He was a young, quiet and very patient person not very well known by the court. He asked Alice to tell him the whole story of her life and about all the abuse her husband had inflicted upon her. She had to tell him about her husband's friend and of the rape of her daughter. Also, that she knew people that knew about her situation. He listened and recorded all she said.

When he left the courthouse, he met Alexander from the newspaper, coming into the building. They had never met before so they introduced themselves, but when Mr. Stanton heard that Alexander was a reporter, he was at first hesitant to make conversation with him. Alexander told Mr. Stanton that he was a good friend of Alice and that he was looking for her daughter. Mr. Stanton (Sean) told Alexander to call to make an appointment because he would like to talk to him. That same day Jim found out from the newspaper the name of Alice's lawyer. He and Ellis had to tell Vince and Conny about it and asked them what to do. They all agreed that Jim would approach Sean Stanton and ask him to take Jim to see Alice.

Back in his office at the newspaper, Alexander took a look at the history of the work of Sean Stanton. He was pleasantly surprised to learn of the excellent record and decency of this person. In the afternoon, Sean received a phone call from Jim with a request to talk to him. It was decided that the men would meet in a quiet restaurant for a cup of coffee. When Jim met Sean, he thought he had seen this man before but he must have been mistaken about this. Sean asked Jim what his relationship was with Alice and Jim told him that before he married and moved to another address, he had lived in the same building as Alice and that he wanted to talk to her. Sean thought it was not a good idea but he would like to know if Jim knew about the husband's abuse toward Alice. Jim told him that it was a long time ago and he never saw anything that he could tell Sean. Jim went home disappointed with the possibility of not being able to see Alice.

Sean worked long hours to find witnesses for his defense in Alice's trial. Many people were interviewed but beside some prostitutes, not much was known about Alice. He knew she had a daughter but nothing was known about her either. Sean phoned Alex at the newspaper: maybe he knew something? Both men talked about Alice but Alex was careful not to mention anything about the package she had given him for Jennifer. Sean told Alex about Jim's request to see Alice and maybe he could find out more about his relationship with her?

Alex thought it was worth a try and Sean offered him Jim's phone number at the hospital. First, Alex did not know what to think about phoning Jim. It could be a risk because he was looking for Jennifer. Maybe he just could pretend that he was interested in Alice's trial? Two days later, Alex decided to phone Jim but he received a message that Jim was at home sick with the flu and they did not want to give his address or phone number over the phone. So, the conversation with Jim would have to wait. At the time, Ellis and Jim were both at home, fighting off the flu.

Time went by. The weather was changing for the better. It was almost winter and the days were shortened and so were the days for Sean to prepare himself for trial. Alice's trial was set for January but Sean had asked for a delay because he had nothing to go by. When he next talked to Alex about Jim, Alex told him he would try again.

The next day, Alex decided to go to the hospital to speak to Jim. When he came into Jim's office, he felt comfortable at first, but when he told Jim that he was a friend of Alice and that he was looking for her daughter, he thought he saw a change in Jim's face. Maybe Jim was afraid of something? Alex told Jim that he had been talking to Sean, Alice's lawyer. He asked Jim why he would like to visit Alice in the jail. Jim told him that he was an old neighbor and was trying to help her. Alex agreed to take a risk with this man whom he thought knew more than he was letting on. So, he told Jim of his friendship with Alice and that he would try to get Jim a visit to the jail so the both of them could talk to her. It was unusual to be granted a visit when you are not a lawyer or family but because Jim was an old neighbor maybe it was a possibility and worth a try? They had luck with the prosecutor because Alex used a favour. That afternoon when Jim finished work, both men went to the jail to see Alice. They were only allowed 10 minutes to talk to her. Alice looked better than before; the rest and the regular meals showed off.

When she saw both men she was surprised and asked Alex about his visit. First, Alex wanted to introduce Jim to her but she recognized Jim and she asked him in a friendly way why he wanted to talk to her. To the amazement of Alex and Alice, Jim said, "I have a message and I think I can help you but I could not tell you about it before I knew that I could trust your friend Alex."

He told Alex that he would tell him later in his office. He could see that Alice was eager to know what the message was but he told her that she had to wait. When Alex and Jim left the jail both men were quiet until they arrived in Alex's office. Most people at the newspaper had gone home and only a few reporters were still there. Alex closed the door to his office and could not wait to ask Jim about his secret message. Jim did not know where to begin but he began in a whisper with the most important answer, as if a block fell of his shoulder, "I know where Jennifer is."

Alex was perplexed. He would not have dreamed about this answer and could almost scream but said in a whisper "Man, I have been looking for her for a long time."

Jim invited Alex to come to his house to talk with him and Ellis in private. There was much to tell and nobody was to know about it until everything was 100% safe for Jennifer. There was to be no phone calls or other communication other than between Jim and Alex. They both agreed about a visit to Jim's house. When Jim came home, he told Ellis all about his visit to the jail and to Alex's office. Both were nervous about it but also relieved and Ellis was asking questions about Jennifer's mother.

For Jim it had been a long day and he could not sleep that night. What would happen when they have to give up the secret of Jennifer's address? He prayed to God to have done the right thing. He was not the only one who had problems to get to sleep. Ellis was thinking about losing Jennifer. She was not living with her but she always felt that she was part of her family and Conny was so happy with Jennifer too.

In the jail, Alice could not sleep either because she was thinking what the message for her would be. She was told not to tell Sean about it. Alice had made some friends in jail. Women who had not done the kind of crime that she had done. The friends she made knew her situation but she would never tell them everything. Anything could happen to hurt her. She had not seen her lawyer for a long time but she was convinced that there was nothing he could do for her. The only thing that was important to her was that she was now safe. Alice was not afraid about what her sentence would be. She had no cellmate and she liked to be by herself. Most of the day she read books, something she had not done for a very long time. In the evening she could watch TV or do some exercises. One of the women's guards was keeping an eye out for her. She was a friendly person who seemed to know what the reason was for the crimes the women had done. But Alice did not trust anybody. She did do her best to be friendly with everyone.

She was wondering about Jim. She knew him from the time when he was living in the same apartment building. He was always happy to see Jennifer and she was not afraid of him when she was a little girl roaming through the corridors. He always had a friendly word for her. Did he maybe know more about Jennifer? Her head was spinning with questions that she could not ask anybody.

Jim and Ellis were waiting for Alex. They had made coffee and Ellis bought some raspberry cake. It was seven o'clock when Alex knocked at the door and Ellis answered it. First, they had coffee and cake. They all were at ease when Jim asked Ellis if he could do the talking, and when he forgets something, to help him. Jim started at the beginning that night when they let Jennifer into their house. At the end, he told Alex that Jennifer was safe and in good hands but that he could not give her address yet before he could prove she would be safe.

Alex knew enough and he was happy to know that these people had done so much for Jennifer, risking their lives to do so. Yes, he felt good to be with such nice people and he promised them he would not tell anybody. He also told them about the package Alice had given him for Jennifer. Jim told Alex that he could tell Alice that her daughter was safe but she should keep it as a secret. After the trial and when Jennifer was ready, she would come to visit Alice. But for right now, the danger was still there.

Chapter 5

Vince, Conny and Jennifer finished their dinner and Jennifer got up to do the dishes. Normally the women washed the dishes together but Vince had to talk to Conny about his trip to Blytonfille to see Jim and Ellis.

Jennifer knew about her mother's trial date and the name of her lawyer. Jim had told her about his visit to the jail, his talk with Alex and the way her mother acted when he told her he had a message for her. Alex would tell Alice that Jennifer was safe. Conny told Jennifer that she would always be safe in their home and that she was like a daughter to her, but she understood that her mother was important, too. Whenever Jennifer felt that she wanted to visit her mother, they would do everything to help her. Conny had tears in her eyes when she spoke to Jennifer of all this. She really wanted Jennifer to stay with her forever. That coming weekend, the house would be filled with people. Jim and Ellis would bring Alex for an important visit to discuss Jennifer and her situation.

It was coming close to December and for the first time in many years, Conny was looking forward to the Christmas holidays. She never had a cozy home-cooked dinner for Christmas. They always went to a party or a restaurant, but this time with Jennifer, she was planning for a real home Christmas. She prayed that nothing would change her plans. The weather was getting cold and snow was in the air. When the visitors arrived, they came into a warm and cozy house. Alex was pleased to meet Jennifer. Everybody was in a good mood as they were seated around the fireplace. Conny thought this would be nice for Christmas too. When the coffee and cookies were served, the talk started and the first thing of importance was the little package that Jennifer's mother had given to Alex for safekeeping. Of course, Jennifer had to open it because her name was on it, but everybody was eager to see what was inside.

In the package was a bundle of money bills, some loose change and two gold rings that had belonged to her father. Jennifer did not want to touch any of it. She told them that she did not want any of this, so please give it back to her mother as she had worked for it. They all understood and asked Alex to see what he could do to make good use of it. Maybe he could pay some of it to the lawyer or hold on to it until the trial was over? Alex asked the family if Sean was allowed to visit Jennifer to ask her some questions about the rape and of the abuse of her mother. Sean would keep it all confidential. They all agreed except, he could not use Jennifer or the address of where she was living in his client's defense. Nothing would be done to put Jennifer in any danger. So, on that, all was decided. Alex and Jim went home and Ellis stayed with Jennifer, Vince and Conny. This was a good time for Conny to talk about her idea for Christmas.

Vince told Conny that he liked Alex and his determination to help Alice. He would keep them informed about the trial. The rest of the day, Ellis, Conny and Jennifer talked about daily things. Ellis had been promoted to a much higher paying job. She told Conny and Jennifer that she would like to have a party to celebrate! They set a date and agreed that it would be at the home of Vince and Conny so that Jennifer could stay safe at home.

Alex, in his office at the newspaper, was going to investigate the places and the people associated with Alice's late husband. Now that he knew about Alice's life, he was going after the people who were involved with her late husband. He was not going to the police because some of them were good friends of the deceased and they were not trustworthy. He talked to Sean and told him about his conversation with Jim and that he could not reveal the message he had for Alice until he knew more about some people.

Alex succeeded in finding information about the man who had raped Jennifer. He had had a wife but no children or other family. His wife moved to a different state and city after their divorce and had married again. So, from that side there would be no trouble. The late husband of Alice had a sister but the two hadn't any contact for many years, and also, she was living in an institution. Furthermore, there were some dubious friends whom Alex was afraid of because there was always the possibility of revenge. When Alex visited Sean, he told him what he knew about Jennifer and the man who had raped her. He also told about the money he received in the package from Alice. He felt that he could trust Sean. He handed Sean the envelope with the money and the rings. Sean did not know what to say at first, but he thought he could not use this money because it compromised the trial. So, he handed the money back to Alex. He said that it was too bad that he could not use Jennifer as a witness but he understood their wishes to keep

Jennifer safe and out of the trial proceedings. He promised to argue in court without mentioning her or even her name. It would not make any difference in Alice's case. However, he asked Alex if he could put a short story in the newspaper about the life of Alice. He said that there must be medical records in the hospital about Alice's broken arms, cigarette burns and other abuse injuries. Maybe Alex could find out from Jim and Ellis or some other way? Alex agreed with pleasure and told Sean to keep their conversation secret.

Two weeks later, Jim read Alex's newspaper story about Alice with much interest. Days after the story, many people wrote to the newspaper about how they were disgusted about the abuse. Some even blamed the police and justice system for not protecting the rights of women. There were even a few women that had protested at the court building. The newspaper had run a good story and Alex was complimented about it. The most important result was the influence to Alice's case. It would certainly make a difference in her sentencing.

Christmas was this week and Conny had her wish - all the men and Ellis were coming for Christmas dinner. Alex and Sean booked a hotel to stay overnight. Much had to be done with cooking and decorating but the warm Christmas atmosphere was there. Sean went to the jail to talk to Alice and he brought her good news and some Christmas gifts.

She was looking much better every day and Sean was hoping that nobody would destroy her life this time. In jail, jealousy can do a lot of harm but Sean would keep in touch with her. Now he had a good friend at the newspaper and knew that printed protests do more good than spoken words.

Jim and Ellis went shopping for the Christmas party. It was busy in the stores and Ellis could not make up her mind. She never had to buy so many gifts, but with the help of Jim and a list, they managed to get what they needed. Ellis bought some new clothes and shoes. When they came home she was tired but satisfied. In Massonville, Conny took Jennifer with her to do the shopping and the main street with all the Christmas decoration looked like a Christmas card. The fluffy snowflakes were coming down and the warm coat Jennifer was wearing made it feel like a dream and she forgot all her worries. When they came home Vince was waiting and he noticed how both women were so happy. Christmas would be great! He was looking forward to seeing the rest of the company. The day before Christmas, Vince, Conny and Jennifer wrapped all of the gifts and put them under the Christmas tree. Music of the season was playing and all looked perfect in their eyes. Tomorrow would be a big day for all of them.

Chapter 6

When Alex looked through the stack of newspapers that he had taken from the archives in order to find some information about a case he was working on, he noticed a story about a policeman involved in a case of blackmail from 18 years ago.

This same story also was talking about prostitution in Blytonfille. He noticed that not much had been done in this case. Alex started to think about the time back when he was still at university studying to become a journalist. One of his fellow students had written an essay about prostitutes. At that time Alex did not have the time or interest to look it over because his parents were not rich and he had to study a lot to finish his education. Maybe he should look into it now and find out more about what this student wrote in his essay. Maybe his friend knew more about the time when this policeman was in trouble?

Alex was tired but he was looking forward to the Christmas party. He liked the people who were involved with the daughter of Alice. He liked Alice, too, and he felt sorry for her. At one time, when he did not know she was married and also a prostitute, he almost fell in love with her, and he was still attracted to her.

Alex took the telephone and dialed the number of his parents to wish them a Merry Christmas. He could not visit them because they were living too far away and it was his turn to be in the office this year. He loved his Mom and Dad. He was their only child and they worked hard to give him a good education. He had booked a flight home to be with them at New Year's Eve.

His mom answered the telephone and he told her that he loved her and asked how his Dad was doing. Everything was fine only they would miss him at Christmas. Alex told his mother about the people he had met and that he was going to their party. He told his mother that he would tell her all about it when he got home. Both his parents were retired and were living in a small town called Chester close to Lake Monrou. They had a small but beautiful house. Alex thought about the time when he was growing up in that little town, and now he was almost 50 years of age. The telephone rang and Sean's voice brought him back to the reality. Alex and Sean would drive to Massonfille together. Sean told Alex that he would pick him up around 5 o'clock in the afternoon at the newspaper office. Alex liked Sean and the drive over would give them plenty of opportunity to talk.

Chapter 7

Sean received a letter from the court that the trial date for Alice was set for the first week of March. He was ready for the trial and had completed 80% of his defense. Sean made an appointment with the warden of the jail in order to see Alice, to prepare her for her court appearance. He also told Alex to be ready for his article in the newspaper and his report on the case. Alex had discovered some interesting facts for Sean that would help him in his defense of Alice. The prosecutor for the state was a woman, and that made it more difficult for Sean, but he had faith in himself.

His secretary had been busy with all the papers necessary for the court procedure and for the prosecutor. Still much had to be done for Alice. She needed clothes and some advice on how to present herself in court. The lady from the Salvation Army had spoken with Alice and would be a witness. Alex had visited Alice twice and he was happy that all was going well with her. He had told her about Jennifer and that she had to wait until later to see her. Alex did not know how to feel around Alice. There was still the love he had for her but could he see her without her past life as a prostitute? Even without her makeup she looked good and healthy. Now he could see the likeness of Jennifer.

He wished he could bring Jennifer to her, since it would be better for Alice's mental condition. Alex would have to talk to Vince and Conny and also to Jennifer about this. He had a better idea, and right away he phoned Conny to talk about what he was planning. He would take a picture of Jennifer to show to her mother the next time he went to the jail. Conny did not like it at first, but then agreed to the idea.

At his next visit, Alex showed the picture to Alice. She could not keep her tears from falling and could not believe her eyes to see the beauty of her daughter. Now the knowledge of what she had done to her daughter was even more painful. Alex felt sorry and told her that maybe everything was going to be better in the future. After the trial was over he would bring Jennifer for a visit.

Later he told Sean about his visit to Alice and the picture he had shown to her. Sean told Alex that he was not that happy about it. Sean asked Alex for the picture so he could keep it in his office. A year from now, that girl in the picture would become an important part of his life…

With the agreement of Vince and Conny, Jennifer was going to do her end of high school exam. They would send in her papers as soon as she was ready for it and they hoped for good results. At some point, Jennifer would have to face the reality of going to find a job to help pay for her stay at the home of her friends.

That weekend they had a surprise visit from Sean. He told Vince and Conny not to worry about the future and that Jennifer would not have to testify in court. When Sean looked at Jennifer he could see how much she had matured since the time he was at their home at Christmas. She was looking so beautiful and she had a great smile. He felt attracted to her.

Driving back home, he had lots of time to think about everything that had happened. Every time there was one picture in his mind that came back between his thinkings on the court case. That picture was Jennifer. It was late in the night when he came home and he was tired from the long drive. The next day he had lots to do because the trial was coming up in two days.

Alex prepared the newspaper article about the upcoming court case and made sure that he made no mistakes. He had to look over his writing very carefully until he was satisfied with the headlines, confident that it would make a good impression for the readers. His boss gave him the final okay. Alex was the senior editor to the paper and he was second to the chief editor. So, the next day there would be an extra edition. On that day, Jim and Ellis were eager to read the story and were pleasantly surprised with the contents. They phoned Vince and Conny to keep them up to date.

Jennifer carefully finished her exam and tomorrow, after a final check, she would send it in the mail. She felt satisfied and good in her heart. Things were going a lot better. She asked Conny if she would like to go for a walk with her in town. She did not feel like a prisoner anymore. Conny said that she would like to go out too. She told Jennifer that they could do some grocery shopping.

The weather was mild for the time of the year and both women chit-chatted on the way into town. Jennifer told Conny that she liked Sean and that he was such a handsome fellow. Conny was surprised but did not say anything.

Later in bed, she told Vince and asked what he thought about it but he said nothing. When Vince was already sound asleep, Conny was still awake and wondering about the future.

The first day in court the prosecutor presented her case and it didn't sound very good for Alice. She presented no witnesses and told the judge that she would redirect her questions to the witnesses of the defense. Court was adjourned until the next day. The public opinion was great and many people were in the courthouse. The jury members were selected and they hoped for a quick trial.

When Sean came back to the office, he had a visit from Jim and Ellis. They were interested in what he thought about the progress but he really could not say anything. Alex was busy that night with his report from the courthouse. His article had to go in the paper for the Thursday morning edition and he had no time for other things. He could not make a visit to see Alice and he did not like that at all. What was the matter with him? Was he still in love with her? He could never be involved with her anymore! Alex pushed the thoughts of her away and concentrated on his work. Tomorrow Sean would present his opening statement to the court. Alex was wondering how he would do as a young lawyer. He liked Sean and he was doing everything to help his young friend.

The next day, people were waiting outside the court building to get the best seats and to hear the defense. They all were hoping the best for Alice. When Sean told the court about Alice's history, and the way everything ended up with the crime that had been committed, some people were talking and silently protesting and some were even crying. The judge ordered people to be silent. Sean presented the judge and the jury with the names of his witnesses. The court was then adjourned until Monday.

The real trial was to begin with hearing from the witnesses and the questioning from both the defense and from the prosecutor. The judge was surprisingly pleased with the young lawyer and the way he had prepared his defense. Sean made his case so clear and emotional that the prosecution was almost out of her own questions to the witnesses.

The exhibits of hospital x-rays had shown Alice's broken bones. The report from Alex told about the ignorance of the police and their relationship with the deceased husband. The brutal and criminal history of the husband, made a deep impression on the jury. The prosecution questioned Alice about the rape of her daughter and the reason why she did not leave her husband. Alice's answer was that she was afraid to tell the police because they had a friendly relationship with her husband and she had no chance to get away without even more harsh punishment. The defense took two days to complete and the final arguments would be made the following Monday.

Alex diligently gathered his thoughts and prepared his report for the paper. He would not allow himself to be interrupted. His part was to give the readers the best impression about the trial. He had to work long hours before he was satisfied with his work. Sean was working equally hard to prepare his final statements to the jury members. He was reading books about similar cases in the past. Sean found himself full of energy and so he worked until the late hours of the night. He had hired a second secretary to help finish all of the necessary paperwork. It was not possible for Julie to do all the work by herself. Everything had to be checked twice. One mistake could be a disaster for the defense! When the work was all done, they went home for a good rest. The next day they would read the papers and all the notes again to make sure no mistake was made.

That Saturday, Ellis and Jim went to visit Vince and Conny and they brought the newspaper with them. Jim told all about Sean and Alex. Jennifer had a difficult time to absorbing all the news about her mother. She felt pity for her but she also felt that she could not forgive her. Maybe later she would change her mind? Her thoughts went to Sean and she wished he was there, too. Jennifer liked Sean very much but she thought that with what he knew about Jennifer and her mother, he would never love her.

Conny asked Ellis and Jim to stay for dinner and for the night. Jennifer had good news because she had passed her exam with the highest grades and that was a reason for a party! Ellis was happy to stay and Jim had no argument about it. They all had a pleasant time together.

The next day, Jim helped Jennifer to put her resumé together for her job applications. In the afternoon, Jim and Ellis had to go back home. The coming Monday would be a day full of tension and hope for Jennifer's mother.

Alice was sitting beside Sean and she was surprisingly calm. The lady from the Salvation Army had prayed with her in the morning and she was sitting behind her in the courtroom. The judge came in the room and they all stood up. The prosecutor was reasonably mild in her final address to the jury but she restated that a high crime had been committed. Alice's hope for any clemency faded away. When Sean started his long prepared final objective statement with all the facts and arguments, a hush fell over the room and his electrifying address to the jury kept everybody's attention. Even the judge was so impressed that he could not take his eyes off the young and brilliant lawyer.

When Sean finished, the judge instructed the jury to think about the crime that was committed and that no personal feelings should enter their deliberation.

It took two long days for the jury to come to a verdict, and when Sean was called to the court, he felt somewhat at ease about what the jury's decision would be.

Alice had already been brought to the courtroom. Alex called Sean, and he hurried to the court. Through the radio broadcast, the people were told about the jury agreement. When the judge asked the jury if they had made their decision their answer was "yes". He asked the foreman to read the decision. He handed the judge his paper and read from his copy:

Count one "Not guilty because of self-defense" and count two "Guilty in a lesser degree because the mental state of the accused in the crime".

Sean told Alice that he was happy with the decision and hoped that the judge would be lenient in his sentencing.

The judge told the court to reconvene the next week for his judgment.

The morning newspaper edition had the biggest sales in many years and Alex's report was the top headline. Alex had worked through the night and slept through the day to get it done. Sean told his secretary, Julie to stay at home the next day. They all had done everything that they could for Alice and now they had to wait. Jim brought the news to Vince and Conny via the telephone. They would be happy when it all was over.

One week later the judge sentenced Alice to one year in jail, minus the time already served, along with 10 years' probation with a monthly evaluation by a psychiatrist at the local hospital. Alice was happy and thankful at the outcome of her trail. She did not know how to thank Sean and Alex for all they had done for her. The people in the courtroom were ecstatic and relieved at the outcome of the judge's decision.

The biggest surprise came the next day when the prosecutor came over to Alice and told her that she would investigate the involvement of the local police with the prostitution. She told Alice not to worry about any revenge from anyone. She could serve her time in the local jail so she could have regular visits from her daughter. The warden of the jail was a good friend of the prosecutor and had told her all about Alice. She congratulated Alice and her lawyer, who had done a very good job. Sean later received a letter of commendation from the judge along with his congratulations.

Chapter 8

Jennifer found a job in a clothing store and was feeling happy and content with her life. This coming Saturday Sean was coming over to see Vince and Conny. Ellis had taken Jennifer to see her mother, Alice, and the visit had not been without emotion. Jennifer was still not used to the situation and did not know how to treat her mother but Ellis told her later that such feelings were normal.

Ellis was hoping that a better relationship in the future was possible between Jennifer and her mother. She knew now how strong the relationship had grown between Conny and Jennifer. Ellis, too, was happy with Jennifer.

When Alex came to visit Alice, he brought her some gifts. He still liked Alice very much and the feeling was mutual for Alice as well. When they were talking about the future, Alex asked Alice if she wanted to stay at his house. He told her that he had two spare rooms and she could cook for him. He would also pay her for her work. While talking to her Alex felt uncomfortable and his face turned red. Alice could have kissed him but she told him that she would think about it, and he should know that her past could destroy his career. She then told Alex about Jennifer's visit and the lady called Ellis. Alex told her what Ellis, Jim, Vince and Conny had all done for her daughter. Alice understood, but in her heart, she was jealous. She did not know that later she would have more friends than she had ever had.

The lady from the Salvation Army came to visit Alice and many things were discussed between them, including the proposal from Alex for Alice to live with him as an intern housekeeper. The lady (Betty) smiled and told Alice that it was a good thing for her because she had known Alex for a long time and he was a good man.

Jennifer visited her mother regularly and the feelings for her mother began to become more normal. They talked about the time ahead when Alice would be released and where she would be living. To the surprise of Jennifer, her mother told her about the decision that she had accepted the offer from Alex to be his housekeeper. When Jennifer told Conny about this, they were both amazed with all the good things that had happened and in such a short time.

Jennifer opened the door when Sean came to the home of Vince and Conny. They both stared at each other. Jennifer's heart was giving her a strange feeling and Sean did not know what to say, she looked so beautiful. He was not used to the feelings he had for Jennifer. Conny said, "Are you both going to stay there forever? Please Jennifer, let Sean come in." Conny knew already what was going to happen between the two of them. They were falling in love and she had to help break the ice.

Sean was 8 years older than Jennifer, and Vince was 7 years older than Conny. Conny wondered how could she make them feel more comfortable with each other?

Sean was happy when Vince took him to the living room for a chat. Vince also had noticed the interest that Jennifer had for Sean and he would like to slow it down a little bit. But could he? There was time enough for romance.

Sean had some things to discuss with Vince about Alice's release and the possibility that Alice was going to live in Alex's house. Not that it was a problem for them except how to accept Alice into their friendship with Alex. Vince told Sean that it was all up to Alex.

Later when Sean went back to Blytonfille, he could not forget the picture of Jennifer. He had been in love once before, with the best friend of his sister. Last year when he was at home for New Years Eve, he had met her again when she had come for a visit with her boyfriend but he didn't feel the same anymore. Sean thought it was the same for both of them. Later he told his mother about Jennifer and had showed her the picture. His mother and father told him that they would like to meet her when he had serious plans.

Sean had spoken to Julie about his feelings for Jennifer because she had noticed the picture at his desk. Julie thought that it was time for Sean to make a decision. He wanted to see Jennifer again and he thought that he could ask Ellis if he could pick Jennifer up for the next visit with her mother. When he took the courage to phone Ellis, (who knew already from Conny about the love interest between Jennifer and Sean), Ellis told him that she was happy to have a break from driving to Massonville, but she told Sean to take good care of her and to never leave her alone. Sean had no problem with that. Ellis would phone Conny about his visit.

Sean could not wait until it was Saturday. He left early in the morning. The weather was great and it seemed that they would have an early spring this year. When he got to the house and was about to knock at the door, it swung open and Jennifer was standing there out of breath and with colour on her cheeks. "Boy, is she beautiful!", Sean mused to himself. Conny was right behind Jennifer. She welcomed Sean inside the house and asked him if he was ready for coffee and cake. Both women were happy but Sean felt nervous. As soon as the coffee had been served, it was up to Conny to break the tension. She said with a smile to Sean, "So, you are taking Jennifer for a visit to her mother? You take good care of her and bring her back to me." Sean still felt uneasy and uncomfortable with both women.

Jennifer was wearing a beautiful dress and her hair was in a ponytail and she looked so young and fragile. He felt blessed to have met a girl like her. He was happy to leave, and he thanked Conny for the coffee and cake. He asked Jennifer if she had everything for the visit with her mother. Jennifer said she did. The plan was for her to spend the night at Ellis and Jim's. Then on Sunday, Sean would bring her back to Massonville.

Driving back to Blytonfille, Sean felt more at ease without Conny and he took the courage to talk to Jennifer. But they both started to talk at the same time and were laughing about it. The tension was broken and the conversation started.

Sean could hear in Jennifer's voice that she was still a young girl. He felt more mature than she was, but he made sure that he did not let her feel that way. They were talking about the Sean's family, where they were living and the other common friends that they had. He told Jennifer that he was happy to see her again. Before they knew it, they had arrived in Blytonfille.

After the visit with Alice, Sean asked Jennifer if she would like to go out for dinner with him. Jennifer was happy to accept and they phoned Ellis to let her know not to wait for them for dinner and that afterwards they would be coming to her house.

They went to a good restaurant where Sean had taken Julie and Tom before. He knew the owner and they were seated in a quiet area away from other customers. The dinner was fantastic and Jennifer was so relaxed and enjoying herself. Sean took her hand and asked her if she would like to go out with him again.

Jennifer's heart almost exploded with joy and she answered, "Yes Sean, I would like that very much!"

On their way to Ellis and Jim's house, she had to control her excitement. Sean stayed at Ellis and Jim's house for a chat and when he left he gave Jennifer a kiss on her cheek. He had promised Ellis that he would come for breakfast. He was already looking forward to the next day. Driving home he almost had an accident because Jennifer was still on his mind. At home, he phoned his mother right away to tell her that he was in love and as soon as he was able, he would bring Jennifer for a visit.

The next couple of weekends he brought Jennifer to Blytonfille to see her mother for a visit. The last time he brought her back home, he told Jennifer that he loved her very much and he took her in his arms and they kissed for the first time. He told her that he would like to take her for a visit to see his family, if Jennifer agreed with his plan.

Jennifer told Sean that she was so happy too, and that she would tell Conny about it.

Both Conny and Jim were already prepared for what was happening with Jennifer and Sean. They liked Sean and they were happy for Jennifer to have such a fine relationship. Conny prayed every night for the young couple. How time had changed so many things! She still recalled the first day that she met Jennifer as a young girl and now she was growing up so fast. Sean had booked the flight for Jennifer and himself to visit his family. He told Jennifer to ask Conny to have everything ready for their trip.

The day before their drive to the airport, Sean would stay over at the home of Conny and Vince. That night at the dinner table Sean had a surprise for all of them. He asked Jennifer if she would like to be engaged to him, and he showed her the beautiful ring that he had bought for her. Jennifer started to cry, she was so over-whelmed. She said through her tears "Yes I will!" and she gave Sean the biggest kiss a woman could give to a man. She then went to Conny and gave her a hug and a kiss.

Vince asked, "What about me?" but Jennifer was already on her way to give him a hug, too. So, they all had a big celebration and they toasted their happiness. When Sean was talking to Vince, Conny and Jennifer snuck out of the room to phone Jim and Ellis about the good news. For sure the women were all crying again about it. Jim told Conny that he would phone Alex so he could tell Jennifer's mother.

The next day when they were driving to the airport Jennifer could barely comprehend her new situation. She felt happy, realizing her new life had started with Sean. She was engaged and that means a wedding in the future, but she did not want to think about all that right now. This would be the first time for Jennifer to fly in an airplane. She was so overwhelmed with all of it that when they were seated in the plane, she had to cry. Sean took her in his arms; he knew what was going through her mind. He consoled her, telling her that all would be fine.

When they landed, Sean's sister came to pick them up from the airport. Sean drove the car home while his sister and Jennifer were sitting in the back seat, getting to know each other. Sean's sister Ellen was two years older than Jennifer and was still single. Hearing the conversation between the girls, he knew they were going to like each other. At Sean's parents' home there was another celebration again and the whole family was happy with the new addition.

Unfortunately, they could only stay for two days and for Sean's mother, it was way too short of a visit! She liked Jennifer and thought that maybe in the future, she would give her the grandchildren she was waiting for.

Chapter 9

Time refused to stand still. The summer had been good for Sean. He had lots of work, so much so that he hired an associate for his office. Julie was still working for Sean as a secretary. Her children were in high school so she was able to work more hours. The new associate was an old school friend of Sean's, and Sean wanted to give him a chance to establish himself as a lawyer in town. He was in a different field than Sean, as his specialty was civil law suits. If all went well, he would stay for one year. Julie would keep an eye on him to make sure that everything was working out well.

Alex and Alice were still seeing each other and there was no change in their decision to live in one house together when Alice's time for release came. There was one thing however, that Alex was not used to. Alice had become a devoted Christian and promised to attend the regular services in the Salvation Army Temple. He liked Betty but what if he was not going to church with Alice? Well, he thought, as long as she is living in his house he would be happy!

Alex told Alice about the engagement and she was so happy for Jennifer. She told Alex that she was hoping that her relationship with Jennifer would get better too. Alex had regular visits with Ellis and Jim and they talked a lot about the friendship they had with Sean, Conny and Vince, and about the relationship between Alex with Alice. They knew that Alex had deep feelings for Alice but also that it would not be easy when people began to learn about it.

So, they had a new idea on how to solve this problem, but it would not be easy for both of them. Alex would find an apartment in Massonville where he and Alice could live together as friends. He could rent a smaller apartment for himself in Blytonfille. It was more money but he could stay over the weekends with Alice. How could he convince Alice about this?

The time soon came for Alice to be released, and it was on a Friday that Alex received the phone call from jail that he could pick her up. He brought Alice to his home and showed her the room he had prepared for her. Ellis and Jim had helped Alex decorate the room and to buy the furniture. The sunlight shined through the window and gave the room a cozy atmosphere. The window looked out over a small garden below. It was Alex's old room but he decided to make it nice for Alice. When Alice saw the room and how cozy the furniture made it seem, she felt at home.

Everything was there for her: a television and a telephone. One door led to a bathroom with a shower. So, this would be her new life. She thanked Alex for his hospitality and put down her small case of belongings. Alex closed the door and left her alone with her thoughts.

Alice looked in the closets and drawers; she found new pajamas and other new clothing bought for her by one of Alex's friends. She sat down in one of the comfortable chairs and she realized that she was tired. She did not know exactly what she felt. She could cry but she had to be strong. Silently she prayed the prayer she had learned from Betty. When she was settled and ready, she went down to the kitchen to look after the cooking. Alex would pay her a small allowance for her work. At first, she refused but he convinced her that she needed some money for herself. Alex said that he would pay the same for somebody else to come and clean his house.

The days went by. Alex found that Alice was a good cook. They did not talk too much at dinner and Alex thought that the relationship between them was not working out so well. Alex however, had joined her everyday with her prayers so he did not think that it was his fault. Maybe she had changed so much and was used to being by herself? Every Sunday, Jennifer and Sean came to visit Alice. Sean stayed with Alex while Jennifer visited with her mother.

It was getting close to Christmas and the winter was already showing its cold days. One night when Alex was sitting on the chesterfield reading a book, he fell into a deep sleep. When he awoke, he had a blanket over him. Alice must have been down when he was sleeping. He went to the kitchen to make tea and when he sat down with his mug of tea, Alice came down and sat beside him. Alex asked her if she wanted a cup of tea but she shook her head. Alex saw that she had been crying. He put his mug down on the table and put his arm around Alice's shoulder. She nestled her head on his chest and sobbed quietly. Alex took some tissues out of the box beside him and tried to dry her tears. After a while he asked her what was bothering her. Alice told him that she wanted to love him but she knew it was not possible because of her past and that her body was so degraded by it. He would always remember it. Alex did not know what was happening to him, but he took Alice's head between his hands and gently kissed her. He told her never to think about it anymore – never, because he loved her so much. He told her that when you have so much faith in your heart you must know that only God could judge a person. No human being could pass judgment, only He, the Almighty.

He told Alice that he always had loved her and that he would take care of her for as long as she let him. Her body was shaking and she held him tighter while she was crying. They held each other until the daylight.

Alex had to go out of town for work that day. When he came home, Jennifer was sitting with her mother in the living room. Something must have happened between them. He did not want to ask so he went to his room. When he came back, Alice was in the kitchen making something to eat for Alex. Jennifer told Alex that Sean and she were doing some shopping and she wanted to drop by to see her mother. She told Alex that she made up with her mother and that she had forgiven her and that they would never talk about the past anymore. Alex could hardly believe what she just said but he was happy about it and gave Jennifer a hug.

When Alice set the table for Alex, he suddenly felt hungry. Alex was never a religious person but now he could fall on his knees to thank God for all their blessings. When Sean came in to pick up Jennifer, Alex asked them to sit down with him at the table, where he took Alice's hand. He asked her to pray for him and for Jennifer, Sean and all of their friends because their happiness was thanks to the goodness of God Almighty. He asked Jennifer to let Conny know that he and Alice would like to come to their Christmas party.

When Sean and Jennifer were gone, he asked Alice to please sit down and when she sat down, he fell on his knees before her. He took her hands and with tears in his eyes, he asked her to marry him and to please accept the ring he had bought for her. Alice took his hand and pulled him beside her and told him that she would marry him. Alice told Alex that they had to wait for a while and to plan a simple wedding in Massonville. Alex said everything would be fine with him as long as she did not change her mind. He put the simple, but beautiful ring on Alice's finger. Alex took her in his arms and kissed her with all his love for her. That night was the first night they shared the bed together. If they had been young Alice would have liked to wait until they were married, but they were adults and Alex had been waiting for a long time for this.

Now Alex and Alice had to make a decision about where to live, but first they had to inform their friends about their happy news. Nobody knew that Alex had proposed to Alice and they were planning to tell their friends at Christmas. They hoped that it would be a good thing to do.

The days went by and Alice was feeling at peace with the Lord and she told Betty about her wedding plans with Alex. They both prayed and thanked the Lord for all his blessings. Alice asked Betty if she would like to be her maid of honour at her wedding. She also told Betty that she would like to give some money to the Salvation Army Christmas collection. Betty said that she would like to be her maid of honour and that she would accept the money with thanks.

Chapter 10

Alex was working on a news story for the Saturday extra newspaper edition when the telephone rang. It was Conny to tell him that they were looking forward to seeing Alex and Alice at the Christmas party. She told him that Jennifer had told her all about what was going on with Alice, and that she was happy that Alex was taking care of her. Vince wanted to know how Alice was doing and how she looked. Vince had never seen her. He only knew everything through Jennifer.

Conny told Alex what to bring to the party and to bring their own presents if they wanted to do so. There would be also a New Year's party at Ellis' home and they were welcome to come to that, too. Alex thanked Conny for her friendship and hospitality and said that he was looking forward to seeing her and Vince again.

That night he told Alice about the phone call and asked her if she had a wish for Christmas. He was not a shopper and he asked if she would like to go out with Jennifer to buy something for her and Jennifer. He also asked her to buy the things for the party. She told Alex that she was afraid to go into town.

Alex then assured her that he would go with her to Massonville because he understood her fear. The weekend before Christmas, they went to do the shopping in Massonville. He had phoned Conny to say that they were coming to pick up Jennifer and at the same time they could stay for coffee and then they could meet Alice. Conny thought that it was a great idea. She was always curious about Jennifer's mother. Jennifer had told Conny that she would like to stay with Conny and Vince until she was married and asked Conny to be her matron of honour. This indeed was a great honour and hard to refuse.

The visit with Conny and Vince went well and both thought that Alex was a lucky fellow with such a nice lady as a friend. Alice and Jennifer did all the shopping without any problems. Some things were bought in the store where Jennifer was working and she was proud to introduce her mother to the other girl she was working with. Jennifer and Sean would not be there at Christmas because Sean had promised his mother to be at home with his family, so Conny had planned the party two days before Christmas. Now everything was ready for Christmas.

When Alex and Alice were at home again, they were both tired and they ordered in some food from the restaurant. After dinner, they went straight to bed because Alex was exhausted, having been so busy with his work. This year, he was taking his holidays at Christmas. He had asked Alice if she would like to meet his parents. He knew that there would be some questions from his Mom and Dad. They knew Alex so well and always thought that he was capable of making his own good decisions. They would be happy for both of them. The only one who was scared was Alice. Her life had changed so much in such a short time, but she knew Alex would take care of her.

Alex booked the flights and asked Alice if she needed anything for their trip to Chester. But she said that everything was ready. First thing the next day, they were going to the Christmas party in Massonville. Both were happy that the weather was still mild for the time of the year. Alice was feeling so good on the drive with Alex. He was always good-natured and sometimes they would sing together. Alex told her about back when he was in school and that he never had time for pleasure. His parents never had too much money and he appreciated all they had done for him.

Alice then told him how she had lost her parents when she was 17 years old. They were in a bad accident. Alice had no other family and had to work in a restaurant to provide for herself. What had happened later in her life, she said that she did not want to talk about it and Alex said he understood. Before they knew it, they were in Massonville

The windows of Vince and Conny's home were pleasantly lit. They found a spot to park the car and carried the presents and other things to the house. When the door opened, Jennifer and Sean welcomed them, wishing them a "Merry Christmas." Inside, you could smell the food that was baking. They were all there and Sean started to play the piano. Jennifer took her mother to the kitchen where Ellis and Conny were finishing the cooking. They all hugged each other and asked Alice about the ride over to Massonville. The ice between the women was broken and Alice felt already a lot better - but what about the men?

When the table was set and the food on the table, nobody was complaining about what they saw. Alex asked if he could say grace and all agreed. The dinner was delicious and there was plenty of laughter. Vince asked Sean when the wedding would be. Sean said that he was still looking for a best man. He asked if maybe Alex would be his best man? Vince said, 'What about me?"

Jennifer said, "No, you have to give me away!"

They all were laughing and the conversation went on to other topics.

When Alex looked at Alice, she told him to tell everybody the plans they had made. They all looked at Alex and there was silence. Alex stood up, took his glass and said that he would like to make a toast. You could see that nobody had any inkling of what was coming. Then Alex told them the news they all were waiting for. He said, "Well friends, I would like to make a toast to my future wife Alice."

First there was a short moment of silence. Then there was the noise of everybody wishing both Alice and Alex happiness; the laughter, the kissing and hugging. Jennifer gave Alex and her mother the biggest hug and she and her mother were crying. Conny took the women to the kitchen and they celebrated the good news with lots of tears of happiness.

In the living room the men had lots of questions about when and where Alice and Alex's wedding would be. When they all were having the coffee and cake, Vince said to Alice, "Alice we welcome you to our friendship and we all wish you both a long, healthy and happy life together".

Sean said to her, smiling, "Take good care of Alex." Until late in the evening they celebrated the best Christmas they ever had. All had fun with the presents they had bought for each other, but the biggest gift of all was their friendship.

Later that night, Alex and Alice left to go to the hotel they had booked. They all wished each other a Merry Christmas and the hugging and kissing took a long time. Tomorrow they would travel to Chester. On the way to the hotel, Alex told Alice that he was so happy with her and that he could not wait to be married to her. Now he had a wife and a daughter and maybe later, there would be grandchildren! In the hotel they both fell asleep and each had their own dreams. Alice still could not believe what had happened to her. She wished that she still could give Alex children but she knew that it was probably not possible.

Chapter 11

Early in the morning they woke up and outside there was a thin layer of snow. The ride to the airport went without incident. They hoped their flight would not be cancelled. But the weather forecast was good and their trip had no delay. When they arrived in Chester, the rental car was waiting, and the ride home took no more than one hour. Alice looked out the car window and noticed the beauty of the country.

It was a combination of forest, small lakes and the road spiraled through the hills. This was very different than living in a city like Blytonfille. She was wondering where Alex' parents lived. Small houses and farms were hidden between the trees. The tranquility of the surrounding area made one feel alone on earth and yet it instilled a peaceful feeling. Alex noticed her quietness and asked her how she was feeling. She said that she was looking forward to seeing his parents and that everything around them was so beautiful.

When they were almost there, they could see the lake and the house where Alex grew up. He was wondering how his mom and dad were doing. His mother never spoke much about his dad. His parents were close to 70 years of age and his Dad had been in a hospital once for a minor operation. They were both very strong and healthy the last time Alex was there. The barking of a dog interrupted his thoughts. Then there he was, Benjamin at the front of the white picketed fence. Alice saw a cozy red-roofed house. Alex said, "Darling, we are almost home."

Alice could not believe her eyes when they stopped at a small garage beside the house. It all looked so beautiful.

Benjamin jumped at Alex when they got out of the car and was sniffing at Alice. Alex's mom opened the door and called Benjamin inside. Mom and Dad welcomed both of them with a big hug and kiss. Alex introduced Alice and told them about the trip. Benjamin liked Alice so much that he did not want to leave her. Alex's mother, Anna, took Alice's hand and showed her the house and the bedroom for Alex and Alice to sleep. She put her arm around Alice when they were sitting on the side of the bed. She said to Alice that she felt so sorry for what had happened to her but at the same time that she was happy for Alex that he had found her. Anna said that she almost thought Alex would never marry and now she would have a daughter. Alice had tears in her eyes and hugged Anna. She thanked her with a big kiss on the cheek. Alex was calling them and asked if they were staying there forever.

When they were sitting in the living room, Alice felt very much at ease. Alex's Dad, John, looked at both of them with a smile and said, "We are so happy that you both are here for Christmas. It gets a bit lonely around here".

Alex took care of their luggage and things they had bought for Mom and Dad. He put it all in the bedroom. When he was standing there in his old room, his mind went to his younger years and all kinds of memories. He came back to the reality when Benjamin jumped on his legs. He loved that little dog he had bought for his mom a few years ago. Alex and Benjamin went down to the living room.

Both women were in the kitchen and Dad asked Alex about the work at the newspaper.

Alex told him about all the friends he had made in the past two years and about Sean, the lawyer and Alice's daughter. He told his dad that he was planning to write a book. The women brought in the coffee and pastry. Alex was ready for coffee and the smell of the homemade baking was mouth-watering. The day was going by fast and the sun was disappearing for the evening.

Where Mom and Dad lived, the days seemed shorter. There was no street lighting and no neighbours close by. Dad told Alex that there was snow coming, so they would have a white Christmas! The house was cozy and the stove in the kitchen gave enough heat for the whole house. Alex told Alice that she would need warm pajamas for the night because the winters were cold in the county. Mom set the table and asked Alex to help her with the dishes.

When they were in the kitchen she gave him a big hug and said that he was a good son and that she was happy with his plans to get married to Alice. Alice gave her a good feeling. She had always hoped for grandchildren but now she thought she was too old for that. She also understood that it was not possible for them to have children.

Alex had never thought about having children. Later he would talk with Alice about it. Strange that he never thought about it. Was it because he was always busy and single? Was it some kind of a hint from his mother? Anna said, "Alex what are you doing? Dreaming? Help me."

John showed Alice some pictures from the time Alex was a schoolboy and it was obvious that his parents loved him very much. He had given them so much pleasure. Alex was their only child and Alice noticed that they were very proud of him. Alice told John that she was an only child too, but that her parents were dead. She asked John if she could call him Dad.

John looked at her and said, "Of course, my dear. I would like that very much and my wife would like it, too, if you would call her Mom."

Alice felt blessed and comfortable with Alex's parents. Both men looked so much alike. John had the same curly hair and sparkling eyes. Could their happiness last? Only the Lord would know.

It was Christmas day and the dinner table was set with candles. Benjamin was lying on his blanket and had already eaten his extra-favourite dog food. Anna's food looked delicious! Alex's father said a short prayer and asked the Lord to bless the food and the hands that had prepared it. They were hungry and did not talk very much until the dessert was served. Alice said that she had enjoyed the meal and thanked Mom and Dad for their hospitality. Afterwards, Alice helped Anna with the dishes and talked about the upcoming weather. Maybe they would have a white Christmas anyway.

Having coffee and cake, they exchanged their presents and wished each other a Merry Christmas. There was a cozy atmosphere and they watched a Christmas television show until it was time to go to bed. John and Anna were used to going to bed early, but on this occasion, they went to bed late.

When they all went to their rooms Alex asked Alice if she needed anything for the night. The nights in the county are a lot colder than in the city. In bed, Alice was lying in Alex' arms and felt the warmth of his body. They fell asleep while outside, the snow was coming down.

Alice woke up with a pain in her left arm. It was the arm that had been broken twice. Alex was still in a deep sleep and Alice did not want to wake him up. She got out of bed to take something for the pain that was getting worse. The doctor from the jail had told her that this was normal when the weather changed. When she had taken some pain pills, she looked out of the window and she could see the winter wonderland under the moonlight and a shiver went through her body. She crawled back in bed beside Alex. Alex woke up briefly and he kissed her and asked her if she was all right. Peace fell over them again.

When Alice woke up in the morning, Alex was already gone. She heard the shower going. She lay in bed thinking about the time she worked in the restaurant when she was a young girl. She had no family and had difficulty paying for her necessities. She had met Chuck Bentons and thought she was in love with this man. He promised her the moon and told her to marry him. From that time her life became a living hell. The day she found out that she was pregnant with Jennifer was one of her luckiest days. After that though, she had more beatings than love. She knew what a big mistake it all had been. She pushed the past from her mind and put on her warm housecoat and slippers.

When Alice went downstairs, Anna was already in the kitchen. The big stove was giving off lots of heat. Anna said, "Good morning, my dear," and asked, "Did you have a good sleep?" Alice said that she had. Anna had baked her own bread in the oven of the big stove. On a plate there were fresh delicious biscuits. Alice was getting hungry. John was out with Benjamin. As soon as he got back they would have their breakfast. Alice went upstairs to get dressed because she still had time.

Both Alex and Alice went down to the dining room. Alice asked Anna if she could help, but everything was ready. Benjamin's nose was white from the snow when they came into the house. John said that he had seen some deer, but Benjamin had scared them away. There was not much snow but the whole world was blanketed in white. Alex asked Alice if she would like to go out later for a walk. Alice really liked that idea. She helped Anna to clear off the table and wash the dishes. Anna was telling how lonely it was in the wintertime and that she had never gotten used to it. When Alex was still at home it was different because there was always laughter and joy. She loved her husband but they had not many friends around so in the winter there was not much to do.

Later, Alice mentioned to Alex what his mother had told her. Alex had never thought about the loneliness of his parents. They had never told him about it. He wondered why they didn't move to a city or at least closer to a city. Alex knew that his dad liked to live where they were, but he thought maybe he could talk to his dad about it.

The walk through the forest was great and Alice had a red-coloured face from the fresh air. Alex had his arm around her and she felt so safe and happy. In her thoughts, she was praying and thanking the Lord for so many blessings.

Back at the house, Mom and Dad were watching the news on the TV, and Alex and Alice were welcomed by the smell of coffee. Alex asked his Mom if she needed something from the store in town. He could drive over and get it for her, but Anna said that she had done all the shopping two days ago. The days after Christmas went quickly and soon they had to go back home to Blytonfille.

Alex had spoken in a diplomatic way to his Dad, asking him if he would like to move somewhere else because it was getting lonely around the house. His Dad probably knew already why all of a sudden this came up. He told Alex that he would like to stay where they were living and that they were all right. Later Alex wanted to ask Alice if she would like to stay with his parents for a while but he thought maybe that was not a good idea.

First, they wanted to get married and after that, they would pay regular visits to his parents. As long as the weather was good, they could visit twice a month so that would make things a lot better for his mother, Anna. On the TV weather channel there was a warning for a winter storm, so Alex phoned his office to let his staff know that they would come back one day later than planned.

When the time came to leave Alex promised his parents that they would visit them as much as possible. Anna was crying when they left but she knew that they were coming back soon. Mom, Dad and Benjamin were waving good-bye to them from the driveway. The next time that they came for a visit, they would be married.

Chapter 12

From the hotel, Sean phoned Jennifer and asked her if she was ready. He wanted to make sure they were not going to be late for the airport. Jennifer told him that she would be ready when he got to their house.

Conny made sure that she had packed all the necessary clothes and that she had not forgotten a warm winter coat for Jennifer. When Sean came to the door grabbed the luggage to put in his car, he saw that Conny and Vince hugged Jennifer and wished them both a good trip. They told Sean to take good care of her. It was the first time that Jennifer was going away from them for almost a week. Conny did not like that too much. Jim and Ellis were still there, otherwise it would be lonely in the house. Jim and Ellis took their vacation from the hospital, and they had accepted the invitation to stay with Conny and Vince. With the holidays, it is better to be with friends than to sit at home by themselves. They were planning to go to a New Years Eve party but changed their minds because the weather was going to change to snow.

On their way to the airport, Sean and Jennifer talked about the plans they had for the coming days. The flight to Sutherland was only two hours and it was on time. Sean's sister did not have to wait long at the airport for them. Sean was looking forward to seeing his family again. During the summer he had been too busy to make many phone calls, but he knew that they were all doing fine. His sister Ellen was going to start her own business selling ladies shoes, hats and other things. She had rented a place in Sutherland and was busy with painting and decorating her shop.

When they arrived at the airport and had retrieved their luggage, they were anxious to know from Ellen how everything was going with her venture. Sitting in the car going home, Ellen told them all about it and invited them to see her shop as soon as they were ready.

Mom and Dad Stanton were happy to see them. It had been a couple of months since the last time they had come to visit. Jennifer met Sean's older brother Michael and his wife Judith. Michael was a lot different than Sean in appearance. He had no freckles on his face and his hair was brown but he had a twinkle in his eye. Judith was a heavy built woman with an easygoing personality. They had no children, and Jennifer was not as comfortable with them as she was with Ellen. Maybe it was because they were older? Later Sean told Jennifer that he and his brother were not so close. They grew up in different ways. Sean went to the university and left home to stay on his own. Michael went to college and lived at home until he married Judith.

Sean and Michael had different friends when they were young, and each went his own way. But they were still good brothers. Michael was a technologist and worked in a factory outside of Chester. Judith was an administrator for a pharmacy in town. They were living in a beautiful house in a new subdivision.

The next day, Ellen took Sean and Jennifer to her store and showed the modifications she had made and all the painting she had done. In the new year she would open the store for customers. Jennifer was surprised with Ellen's energy. She thought that she would never be capable enough to do such a task!

Jennifer, Sean and Ellen decided to go for a coffee and pastry at a next-door coffee shop. Ellen knew the owner because he had helped her a couple of times. They didn't dawdle long as they knew Mom and Dad were waiting for them. Tomorrow would be Christmas and Mom wanted them at home. Michael and Judith were going to a friend's place for Christmas, but they were coming back for New Year's Eve. They wished Sean and Jennifer a Merry Christmas when they left. Christmas was cozy in the Stanton's house. Ellen asked Jennifer and Sean when they were going to be married. They had lots of thoughts about it but had made no plans. Sean said that he would like to be married in his hometown, Sutherland. They had friends in Blytonfille and in Massonville. Since the matron of honour lived in Massonville, there would be lots of traveling involved. Sean had not made a decision yet about who would be his best man. He was thinking about Alex or maybe his brother Michael.

There were some other things he realized. Jennifer had the last name of her criminal father and that could be a problem. When a newspaper got to know about the wedding and found out the name, they could make it into a sensational news item. Sean did not want that kind of publicity for him or for his parents. So, Sean asked Jennifer if he could change her last name, with her permission. She gladly gave to him. They acquired all the necessary documents and Sean would take care of it. The name change could take a long time, so their wedding plans had to wait until then.

Sean and Jennifer went to visit Michael and Judith and met some of their friends. They had a good time. The women watched the TV and the men were playing a card game. Judith took care of all the snacks and drinks, and before they knew it, it was time to go home.

Sean told his parents that he really wanted to go home for New Year's Eve because he had to prepare some administration work for an upcoming court case. He promised his parents that they would come back soon for a visit, maybe for the opening of Ellen's store.

The next day they stayed at the house and Mom taught Jennifer some cooking tricks. She was making finger food for New Year's Eve and some of it was for Sean and Jennifer to take home. Ellen could not wait to get her hands on some of the delicious cookies. Dad watched the girls with a smile. He hoped that the New Year would bring all that they wished for. He was happy with his family.

The day came when they were to leave. They wished a Happy New Year to Michael and Judith when they came to say good-bye. They hugged and kissed Mom and Dad. Ellen drove them to the airport, where they had to promise to stay in touch via the telephone. Ellen said that she would miss them. With a big hug and a kiss, they wished each other all the best for the New Year and a safe trip home.

Chapter 13

The New Year started with a winter blast. Sean was happy that he had come home the day before. Some flights were cancelled and the roads were not that good for traveling, either. From home, he had phoned Julie not to come to the office. The snow was coming down heavily and the wind was picking up strength.

Sean was thinking about Alex and Alice. He hoped that they did not have to travel home today. Sean picked up the telephone and dialed the newspaper and Alex's extension number, but he did not get an answer. Today he would request the papers for the name change for Jennifer. He wished that it were not necessary because it would delay their wedding plans, but Sean knew that they had plenty of time for that because Jennifer was still young. He had asked Jennifer to take a physical exam so to make sure that she was healthy. His doctor would refer her to a good female specialist.

When he was thinking about Alex he thought that it would be difficult for Alice to change her last name because her past conviction, but maybe he was wrong. It would be better for his friend because when people got to know the relationship he had with Alice it could destroy his career. Sean could ask for some information discreetly, but first he would talk to Alex and ask his opinion.

In the afternoon he had a telephone call from Jennifer and she said that she had an appointment with a specialist for an exam. Jennifer was at home with Ellis and Jim. They both would travel to Massonville to bring Jennifer to

Vince and Conny. She would stay there until they were married and Sean would visit on the weekends. It was a drag but Jennifer had to work and she liked her job. This was good for Conny because she was so used to having Jennifer at her home.

Chapter 14

In the office, Alex found a message from Sean, asking him to phone him as soon as he was back. Alex was wondering what his young friend had up his sleeve. But first, he must take care of the newspaper edition. There were some urgent news articles that needed his attention. This would take most of the day but later that night at home he would phone Sean.

Alex met with his chief editor, because there was a case of a missing person and he knew this person. He remembered that name from a domestic fight with police involvement. It had to be further investigated and one of the reporters at the newspaper had to be instructed. There was something strange with this case and Alex did not want to be involved. The whole day he was thinking about what was wrong but could not put his finger on it. It was time to go home and he was looking forward to a cozy dinner with Alice. Before, he did not care how long he worked in the office, but lately he was happy to go home as soon as it was 5 o'clock.

After his dinner, he dialed Sean's phone number. His friend told him about his thoughts about a name change for Alice. Alex had to think for a moment and realized that he had never considered this. He asked Sean if he could take some discreet information and he thanked him for his thoughtfulness. He asked him about his trip to Sutherland and how his family was doing. Alex told him about his flight delay and the time spent in Chester. There was not much to talk about. They were both busy in their respective offices and they promised to get in touch as soon as something new came up.

Chapter 15

Months went by and the winter changed into spring. Alex and all of the friends were occupied with their work. Other than an occasional phone call, life went on until Sean brought the good news to all of them. Sean and Jennifer had finally set the date for their marriage. Jennifer had a new last name approved by the government. For Alice the name change would come a bit later. The female prosecutor from her court case had done some investigating and had asked Sean to do the necessary paper work. She also thought that there would be no problem with the name change. Alex was happy for the help of his friend but insisted on paying for his work.

Sean and Jennifer planned their wedding in Sutherland on a Saturday in July. All their friends had promised that they would be coming. Vince and Conny would stay at the hotel with Jim and Ellis, since they would be traveling together. Vince would be driving because he had a more comfortable car. Alex and Alice would stay at Alex parent's home and they would be arriving on the day of the wedding. After the wedding, they would be traveling to Chester for a visit. They were visiting John and Anna regularly and Anna always looked forward to their visits. She and Alice had become good friends. John was an avid hunter and when they visited, he liked to take his son into the woods for a couple of hours. That way Anna was not alone and they both could enjoy some leisure time.

Alex and Alice were married in Massonville. They had a small but cozy wedding with their close friends. Betty was Alice's maid of honour, and Sean had the honour of walking Alice down the aisle. Alex had arranged for a private dinner in a good restaurant. They all had a wonderful time and they were happy for the newlywed couple. Now they were looking forward to the wedding of Sean and Jennifer. Lots would still have to be done; buying dresses for the wedding party, flower arrangements and many other things. Jennifer had lots of help from Conny and Ellen. The official opening of Ellen's shop was coming up that weekend. She invited everyone to come and told everybody that she had some good deals for the first buyers. Conny and Jennifer were excited because Vince promised to drive them to Sutherland. Maybe they could find beautiful shoes for the wedding or just have a lovely day trip. Jim and Ellis would drive with Alex and Alice to Sutherland.

They left early on Saturday morning. The weather was just perfect for a drive through the county. The ladies were talking about the upcoming wedding and the future of all of them. Halfway through the trip, they stopped for coffee and something to eat. The simple and small restaurant had a surprisingly large menu with a family style of service. After their stop, they still had close to two hours to drive. Sutherland was a mid-size town with close to a hundred thousand inhabitants. When they arrived, it was not easy to find the street where Ellen had her store, but after a policeman gave them the directions, they ended up in the front of a small plaza. The name of the store, "Ellen's Hats and Apparel" captured their attention. The store was quite beautiful and there were already a few customers inside when they entered. Ellen had hired an assistant for the opening day. Alice and Ellis were guided along the racks of clothes and hats and were recommended the special sales. Jim and Alex decided to go next door for a cup of coffee to pass the time while waiting for the ladies.

It took the ladies a long time but they found some good deals on shoes and Ellis bought a beautiful summer dress with a lovely hat.

After wishing Ellen the best of luck with the opening of her store, they went for a sight-seeing tour through the town of Sutherland. They also made a visit to the home of the Stanton's. Later that night they met their other friends, Vince and Conny, in the lobby of the hotel where they had booked a room for the night. The next day they were all to travel home again.

The next time they came to Sutherland, to attend the wedding of Sean and Jennifer, they would have no problem finding their way through the town.

Chapter 16

Alex and Alice were still living in Alex's apartment and their plans to stay had not changed. The chief editor of the newspaper was going to retire and the newspaper was sold to a new owner. As a result, things were going to change for some of the people working in the office. Alex would keep his job as a deputy chief, but his responsibilities were extended and he had to work long hours. When he was talking with Alice about his work, they decided that Alex would look for a new job and a different newspaper to work for. It would be a new life for both of them.

Sean and Jennifer's wedding was going to be this coming weekend and everybody was ready for the trip to Sutherland. Vince, Conny, Alex, Alice, Ellis and Jim had booked rooms in the same hotel where they had stayed before.

Sean had chosen his brother as his best man and Vince was walking Jennifer down the aisle to give her away. Ellen, Ellis and Judith were bridesmaids and they were all fired up for the big day.

The wedding took place in a lovely city hall pavilion in a beautiful garden full of flowers. The weather could not have been better and they all took lots of photos. Alice could not hold her tears and she asked Alex why she deserved such happiness, but Alex just put his arm around her shoulder and could not give her an answer.

Later when they all went for dinner, Alice had a big surprise for Alex. She told him in private that he was going to be a father and that she would see the family doctor as soon as they were back home for an official check up.

He could not keep this joy inside and when he talked to Sean and Jennifer, he told them the great news. Jennifer was so happy and she gave Alex a big hug. She said to him, "I have a great new father and now I will have a brother or sister!"

Later in the hotel bar they celebrated the news with their friends. The wedding was the last time that all the friends would be together.

Conny would be without her beloved Jennifer, but Vince was soon to be retired so the emptiness in her home would not be for long. Jim and Ellis would move to Massonville as soon as Jim retired as they wanted to be close to their friends.

Epilogue

Alex and Alice moved to Byron City in Chester County, closer to his parents. Alex accepted a job with a large newspaper in this city. His work was more professional and the hours at the office were more regular. Alice had permission to have her regular meetings in the local hospital to finish her sentence. They bought a lovely house outside the city. In time, they had two children, a boy Alexander and a girl Alicia. Anna and John were the luckiest grandparents.

Sean and Jennifer bought a house in Sutherland. They have three children; two girls, Ellen and Conny, and a boy Sean Jr. Sean established himself in Sutherland as defense lawyer and rented a new office in a busy section of the city. He missed Julie, his secretary in Blytonfille, but life goes on. Jennifer was content being at home and looking after her family. Grandma and Grandpa were enjoying the children when they came over for a visit.

Ellen was still single and she enjoyed being a shop owner. She did very well with her business. She enjoyed the little time she was free to take Sean and Jennifer's children out for ice cream. They liked their Aunt Ellen very much.

Everything had turned out very well for Jennifer and her mother. They both enjoyed their now extended family and all their friends. This is a happy ending for two women who deserved it. God has definitely blessed them very much.

The End